Sink or Swim

Titles in
the Storykeepers series

Episode 1   Breakout!

Episode 2   Raging Waters

Episode 3   Catacomb Rescue

Episode 4   Ready, Aim, Fire!

Episode 5   Sink or Swim

Episode 6   Starlight Escape

Episode 7   Roar in the Night

Episode 8   Captured!

Episode 9   A Story for Nero

THE STORY KEEPERS

Sink or Swim

Brian Brown and Andrew Melrose

ZondervanPublishingHouse
Grand Rapids, Michigan

A Division of HarperCollinsPublishers 1997

For Abbi and Daniel

Contents

1
A Stormy Night 7

2
Puppet Show 10

3
Suffering Slaves! 15

4
Time for Pantomime 17

5
Do You Know My Father? 20

6
Shark Meat 25

7
Stowaways 27

8
Jump to It 30

9
Nautical Nero 33

10
With the Slaves 35

11
Supper for Stouticus 41

12
In the Soup 44

13
Collision 48

14
Into Battle 50

15
Sinking Slaves 53

16
Ben, Look Out! 56

17
Shark Fin Soup 61

Chapter 1

A Stormy Night

A strong gale blew across the bow and waves lashed the side of the Roman Navy ship. All hands, slaves and soldiers, scurried along the deck, battening down anything that moved as the wooden ship rolled in the heavy seas.

"Hard to starboard," growled Captain Hadrian above the rumble of thunder. "We're in for a real storm tonight."

A large wave washed over the ship, drenching everyone on deck. Lightning crackled across the sky and the thunder that followed shook the ship.

Captain Hadrian leaned into a doorway, which led down a steep stairway to the lower hold where the slaves were rowing. "Guard!" he shouted, as he took a few steps down. He pointed to a hard-faced, evil-looking man holding a whip. "You! Secure the slaves."

"Aye, aye, Captain," said Hard Face.

The captain stood watching. Soon a familiar jangling could be heard as the guard began drawing chains through the shackles on the legs of the rowing slaves.

"Captain, please," said one of the slaves in a pleading tone, looking up at the Captain Hadrian. "We—we'll drown!"

"If this ship goes down, you'll go with it, slave," the captain snapped back angrily.

While Captain Hadrian was below deck giving his order to chain the slaves, on deck a slave named Titus saw his opportunity to escape. Titus was lashing down a row of barrels when the ship gave a lurch and the barrels pitched forward, sliding on the deck. Nervously looking over his shoulder, Titus shoved one of the barrels overboard into the churning sea and jumped in after it.

The waves quickly tossed the barrel, lifting it like a chip on the sea. The wind caught the barrel and began blowing it away from the ship.

Titus surfaced near the ship. One large wave washed over his head, then another, and another. Salt water burned down his throat and stung his eyes. Fighting to get his breath, Titus looked frantically for the barrel. Then he saw it, propelled by the wind and the waves, moving swiftly away from the ship. He swam as hard as he could, his thin legs kicking and flailing to stay afloat. But each time he came close to the barrel, a wave picked it up and tossed it further away.

Help me, Jesus! Titus prayed.

Then a wave came and lifted Titus, carrying him straight for the barrel. His cold, thin fingers closed over the rim. He pulled the barrel to him and with a final heave, pulled himself onto the top, clinging frantically to the slippery wood. He was safe—for now.

Back on the ship, Captain Hadrian, intent on the storm, took over the tiller. The storm's force was still strong. But the wind had changed directions. The ship was now charging into the waves, green water washing over the bow and running the length of the deck on each side before spilling off and returning to the sea.

Titus, clinging to the barrel as it bobbed up and down in the water, watched as the Roman Navy ship sailed away. No one had seen him jump overboard. No one had seen him clinging to the barrel in the water. As he watched, the ship finally became a speck on the horizon, then disappeared into the night.

For the time being, Titus was free. The storm still raged around him. He was far from land.

Titus hoped the wind—the howling wind—just might be his friend, bringing him to shore—and freedom.

Chapter 2

Puppet Show

Later that night, the wind howled and rain lashed at the windows of a bakery in Rome. Snug and warm inside, Ben the baker and his wife, Helena, were putting away the last of the pastries that Ben had made that day. A few pans of rolls were still baking in the oven.

Their work almost done for the day, Ben and Helena wearily sat down to watch the children put on a show. Justin, Cyrus, and Anna had built a small theater out of some old boxes. Little Marcus, Justin's four-year-old brother, was operating the stage curtain. All the children had come to live with Helena and Ben after losing their parents in the great fire of Rome.

"And now," said Justin, the announcer, giving a wave of his hand with the theatrical flourish of a thirteen-year-old, "just back from entertaining the governor of Macedonia, I give you the MAR-velous, the WON-derful, the sen-SA-tional Cyrus and the a-MAZ-ing Anna, who will juggle six rolls!"

10

"Six!" hissed Anna, backstage. "I can't juggle six!"

Cyrus, a young juggler from Africa, pulled a tray of hot, steaming rolls out of the oven and tossed six of them toward nine-year-old Anna. "That's what you think, Anna! Here, catch."

Right on cue, Marcus raised the curtain as the rolls went flying through the air. Anna caught them, one by one, and immediately started juggling. "Ow! Yow! Hot! Hey, Cyrus, I'm doing it! I'm doing it!"

"I knew you could," giggled Cyrus, as Anna tossed the hot rolls to stop them from burning her fingers.

Justin turned to the audience and said, "Now that, ladies and gentlemen, is what I call 'hot-tossed buns.'"

Ben and Helena laughed and clapped, as did Marcus, who got carried away and let go of the rope, accidentally dropping the curtain on the performers. Anna and Cyrus became entangled and fell over in a heap.

Marcus pattered over to them. "Sorry," he said cautiously, keeping his distance until he noticed that Anna and Cyrus were giggling.

"And now for our main attraction!" called Justin, as order was restored. "A story from the Amazing Ben the Baker and his beautiful wife, Happy Helena."

The children cheered as they took their seats, making way on stage for Ben and Helena.

"Thank you, thank you," said Ben as the applause died down. "You know, your show has reminded me of a man Jesus talked about."

"Why, was he a juggler too?" asked Helena.

Ben laughed. "No, no. But he did put on a show every time he prayed."

Helena produced a little hand puppet and said, in a little puppet voice, "Me? Surely you can't be talking about me!"

The children giggled as Ben picked up two other puppets and put them on his hands. "You see, among the people who were interested in what Jesus said were religious men called Pharisees."

"Whee! I'm a Pharisee," said Helen, again in a puppet voice, as she made her puppet look extra pious.

The children all laughed again.

"They were very religious men," continued Ben. "They worked very hard at doing the right thing, but sometimes they overdid it. Some would listen to Jesus speaking, but others would stand away from him, off to one side, praying out loud and making a great show of their devotion.

"One day, Jesus told a story and made sure the Pharisees were listening.

"Jesus said: 'Two men came into the men's court of the temple to pray. One was a Pharisee. The other was a tax collector who worked for the Romans. The Pharisee stood on his own where he thought he would be noticed.'"

"Oh, Lord," said Helena, in her Pharisee puppet voice. "I thank you that I am not like other people! Greedy, dishonest, and wicked. Or like this tax collector."

"The tax collector," said Ben, "looked down in shame as others looked over to where he stood."

Helena continued with her Pharisee act. "I fast twice a week, and I give a tenth of all I earn to the temple!" Helena made her puppet's arms stretch out, piously.

"And," continued Ben, "while the Pharisee prayed, the tax collector wouldn't even look up. Instead, the tax collector beat his chest in shame and kept his eyes on the floor. 'Oh, God, have mercy on me,' he said. 'I know I'm no good!'

"But he was wrong. Jesus told the people that it was the tax collector, not the Pharisee, who went home forgiven."

Helena's puppet looked up, indignantly, as she spoke again in her Pharisee puppet voice. "What? Do you mean *he* is the one forgiven? That—that tax collector? I prayed the loudest!"

The children all laughed as Helena made her puppet look angry.

Everyone was having a good time, just like any happy family, when suddenly there was a knock at the door.

"Goodness," said Helena, as she looked out of the window at the rain. "Who can that be?"

The children were frightened. They had heard late-night knocks at the door before—when they were living with their parents. They knew what could happen.

After the Emperor Nero set fire to Rome, their parents

had been rounded up and taken away by Roman soldiers. Their homes and parents gone, they had been living on the streets of Rome when Ben and Helena had taken them in to live at the bakery.

"Everyone stay calm," said Ben, as he walked to the door. "Who is it?" he called.

"Ben?" whispered a soft voice.

Ben opened the door, but he couldn't see anyone in the darkness. Just then, lightning cracked and the whole sky lit up. Ben saw a shadowy figure lying just outside the doorway. The man had drawn an ichthus—the sign of the fish—in the dirt by his head before passing out.

The children all gasped.

Ben said, "Titus?

Chapter 3

Suffering Slaves!

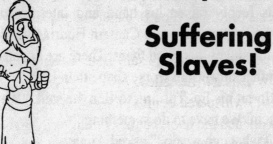

Titus was sitting up in Ben's and Helena's spare bed as Helena mopped his brow with a damp cloth. Nearby, Justin held a water jug. Anna was bringing in hot soup and bread. Titus was telling Ben and Helena and the children what had happened, how he had escaped from the slave ship. And how he had come to be on the ship in the first place.

"After Nero's fires," he said weakly, "when Nero was rounding up all the Christians, I was in a group of men who were sentenced to life on a slave ship … if you can call it a life, that is."

"Oh, Titus," said Helena.

Justin put his arm around little Marcus and pulled him close. "Our father is on a slave ship," he said to Titus. "His name is Joshua Ben Judah. Do … do you know him?"

Titus shook his head. "Son, there are hundreds of ships and many of the slaves are Christians."

"But still, he … he could have been on your ship—" Justin began hopefully.

Titus feebly raised his hand and interrupted Justin. "You should pray he's not. Captain Hadrian would rather starve his slaves than feed them. There are dozens of men still on that ship, all in worse shape than I am."

Justin bit his lip. Turning to Ben, he said, "We have to help them. We have to do something."

"But what can we do?" asked Anna.

Ben smiled at her. He paused, as if working out a plan. "We're going to do what we can with what we have." Then, with a sly grin beginning at the corners of his mouth, he said, "I think it's time we took our show on the road."

Anna and Justin exchanged glances, mystified. They had no idea what Ben meant, but they soon would.

Chapter 4

Time for Pantomime

Down at the docks, families were milling around, greeting the soldiers from the fleet that had just returned. A banner read, "WELCOME HOME HADRIAN THE RUTHLESS."

Ben and the gang had boarded one of the ships, disguised as a theatrical troop, and started to entertain the soldiers and sailors. Dressed in colorful outfits, they were already in the middle of their show. The soldiers and sailors had formed a semicircle on deck, and were watching as Cyrus and Anna finished juggling.

"Hup!" shouted Cyrus with a final flourish.

"And that is what I call 'hot-tossed buns,'" joked Justin, again the announcer.

The audience laughed and applauded as Anna and Cyrus, holding hands, took a bow.

"And now," Cyrus shouted, "a tribute to your glorious victory!"

The soldiers smiled and patted each other on the back

as Justin, Ben, and Zak, Ben's sixteen-year-old apprentice, all wearing raggedy uniforms, appeared in a makeshift boat on a set of colored paper waves. Cyrus and Helena rustled the paper waves to make them look more like water.

They began singing:

> *We are the mighty Icenians.*
> *We sail the open seas.*
> *No Roman ship can stop us.*
> *We just do as we please!*

At the end of the song Ben, casting a look offstage, feigned surprise: "Uh! Oh! It's the unbeatable!"

"The undefeatable!" added Zak.

"Not real sweetable!" sang Justin.

"Hadrian the Ruthless!" they all chorused.

Onto the stage came little Marcus, dressed as Hadrian. He was riding Thastus, his pet goat, who was dressed up to look like a ship. The soldiers all laughed and cheered.

"Hear! Hear! For Hadrian!"

"Retreat!" called Zak.

But as he, Ben, and Justin turned, they became tangled up.

"Ramming speed!" called Marcus in his best Captain Hadrian voice, as he and Thastus charged into the waves. Marcus hoisted his breadstick sword over his head. Thastus snorted and bumped into Ben and Justin. They pretended to swoon, then sank melodramatically beneath the briny paper waves. But they had really disappeared through a hatch that led to the ship's lower deck.

Marcus turned his attention to Zak. "Charge!" he called out.

"But wait, I'm the officer!" Zak protested.

Thastus, suitably unimpressed, butted Zak over the side of the ship. There was a short pause, then a loud splash. The soldiers burst into laughter and loud applause.

Marcus took a bow. Then, like the pantomime expert he was, little Marcus milked the applause for all it was worth. Thastus just stood there, chewing one of the paper waves.

While Marcus was keeping the soldiers busy, Zak swam along the side of the ship and pulled himself into a small boat he had tied there. Then he knocked on a porthole, which popped open, revealing Ben and Justin. Zak began handing them food from a large sack which they had stowed in the small boat earlier.

The juggling and singing and pantomime on deck had just been a diversion for this much more important task: feeding the starving prisoners.

Chapter 5

Do You Know My Father?

Below deck, Ben stacked the food Zak had passed through the porthole. Justin pulled open a trapdoor above the hold of the ship. Ben quickly tied a rope to a heavy table leg and began lowering Justin, carrying a sack of food, down into the hold.

"Be careful, Justin," said Ben cautiously.

Justin descended into the wet, dark hold. A dank mustiness caught at the back of his throat as he breathed. The smell was putrid. His feet touched the bottom, which was covered with slimy water. It was a different world from the rest of the ship.

As Justin's eyes adjusted to the darkness, he managed to pick out the silhouettes of men, all huddling against one another, many of them asleep. These were the slaves. Some were moaning.

He moved cautiously through the gang of men and began handing out the loaves of bread he had brought in his sack. The men reached out hungrily as Justin's eyes moved from face to face.

"Dad? Dad?" he called.

One man, named Andrew, sat up, startled. He was a tough-looking, brawny man, with a black beard and dark, penetrating eyes.

He angrily grabbed a piece of bread out of Justin's hand and began to eat, shoving the bread hungrily into his mouth. Justin drew back in fright.

"What are you doing here, boy?" the man asked gruffly.

"I'm … I'm looking for my father."

"Well, the only thing you will find here is trouble," the man snarled at him. "Now go, before you get us all killed."

* * *

On the upper deck, Cyrus was still entertaining the troops. As he juggled high up in the rigging of the main mast, hanging upside down, a messenger pushed his way through the crowd of soldiers.

"Captain!" he called out. "Captain Hadrian! One of our ships has been taken in a slave revolt!"

He handed Captain Hadrian a sheaf of papers. The Captain read how the slaves on one of the emperor's imperial ships had overpowered their guards, seized the ship, and made their escape. They were last seen headed down the coast, toward the open sea.

He also read his orders from Nero: "Set sail at once and catch the ship before it reaches the open sea or …"

Captain Hadrian didn't read any more. He rose to his feet and called out, "Sound the battle alarm! Cast off immediately!"

A bell began clanging loudly. Soldiers and sailors rushed to their posts, deserting Cyrus, who was in the middle of his act.

"Wait!" called Cyrus. "The big finale's coming up!"

But everyone ignored him.

* * *

While the soldiers rallied to Captain Hadrian's call to arms, Justin, still in the ship's hold with the slaves, looked squarely at the brawny Andrew and said, "My father, Joshua Ben Judah, do you know him?"

Andrew just leered at Justin as the other slaves grabbed for more bread. No one seemed interested in anything except the bread. Suddenly a hatch opened and a soldier peered in.

"All slaves to oars!"

The slaves scrambled for the ladder, running past Justin, and out the hatch, in a blur.

"Wait!" said Justin. "Has anyone seen my father? His name is Joshua Ben Judah."

A haggard old slave, who went by the name of Caleb, stopped for a scrap of bread and said, "He's not on this ship, boy."

Fighting through the chaos of the scramble, Ben stuck his head down through the hatch. "Justin! Grab the rope and I'll pull you out."

"Ben!" Helena shouted, frantic with fear. "They're untying the lines. We're going to be trapped on board!"

Ben tugged at the rope he had lowered into the hold, and up came Justin toward the opening in the deck.

* * *

Zak, standing in the small boat he had tied to the Roman Navy ship, was trying to untie the knot he had made. As he worked to loosen the knot, the slaves shoved their oars out the side of the ship. One oar was right next to Zak. He ducked, but not soon enough. On its swing, the oar hit Zak on the head. He reeled backward, falling on his back in the boat, one leg becoming entangled in the rope.

* * *

Back on deck, Ben, who had heard all the commotion, called out to Helena, "What's happening?"

Helena looked over anxiously. "We're going into battle, that's what, if we don't get off this ship right now!"

Cyrus, looking out over the side, shouted, "It's too late! Look!"

They all turned to see the ship pulling away from the dock.

"Don't worry," said Ben confidently, "Zak's waiting for us in the small boat."

They peered over the side to see Zak sitting in the boat, trying to untangle his leg.

"Ben, hurry … aaaahh!"

"Zak!" shouted Ben.

As the Roman Navy ship picked up speed, the rope around Zak's leg pulled taut and jerked him out of the boat, feet first, into the water. Ben and the rest of the gang watched in horror as Zak was pulled through the water. If he didn't untangle himself quickly, he would surely drown.

Chapter 6

Shark Meat

Back in the Imperial Palace, Emperor Nero was very angry at the bad news. "How dare they?" he ranted. "How dare those slaves steal one of my ships?"

"Indeed," grovelled the weasel-faced Snivilus, Nero's chief toady.

"I'll bet Christians are at the bottom of this," said Nero. "I always said they were trouble. Ever since they came to Rome they have been trouble. They even set fire to Rome."

Snivilus cringed closer to Nero. "Absolutely, Caesar. It was the Christians who set fire to Rome and you are right to punish them. How right you always are."

Nero wrung his hands together and gnashed his teeth; he was very, very angry. "I should have fed them all to the lions. Instead I am kind to some of them. I feed them and gave them jobs as oarsmen with the Imperial Fleet. And now this is how they repay me, by revolting."

"Revolting!" agreed smarmy Snivilus.

"Revolting, indeed," added Nero. "But this time those revolting Christians will all pay. Hadrian, my trusty sea captain, will have them all drowned. I have given my order."

"Hadrian will make shark meat of them all," sniggered Snivilus.

"Shark meat," repeated Nero, with a grin. "Yes, that is a nice thought, Snivilus."

"Ah, but only the best ideas come from Caesar." Snivilus was really beginning to enjoy this conversation, when suddenly, Nero looked a little sad.

Nero pouted. "Oh, but I will miss all the fun. I want to see the sharks eating the Christians. Oh why do I miss all the fun? I suppose it's too late to catch Hadrian now."

"Well, y–yes" said Snivilus. He hated being the bearer of bad news. "H–Hadrian has already received his orders and has set sail."

"And I did so want to see the sharks eating the Christians," mumbled Nero.

Snivilus looked on anxiously. He knew he would have to do something to cheer Nero up. Or else! But he had an idea.

Chapter 7

Stowaways

Zak surfaced and gasped for breath. He was beginning to weaken. He'd already been dragged under the water several times, and he was coughing and choking. He couldn't untangle himself.

Ben and Cyrus climbed over the side of the ship and, letting themselves down on a rope, dropped down into the small boat, which was still tied to the ship. They grabbed the rope ensnaring Zak's leg and pulled him in. Zak was exhausted. But at least he was safe. For the moment.

But now he wasn't the only one in a jam. Captain Hadrian's First Mate, who had been watching from the deck, ordered the soldiers to haul the trio aboard.

Ben, Cyrus, and Zak stood in a line before the First Mate, water dripping from their clothes and making puddles on the deck. Next to them were Helena, Anna, Justin, and little Marcus. And Thastus, the goat, chewing another paper wave.

"Take them below," the First Mate ordered. "Lock them up."

They were under arrest!

Surrounded by burly soldiers, they were marched off to a large cabin at the stern of the ship.

A few minutes later, the First Mate opened the door to the cabin and, glowering at them, said, "The captain will deal with you shortly." He closed the door and locked it.

The children looked around at the elegant quarters. The bed was spread with luxurious linens, and the cabin itself was freshly painted in beautiful shades of blue, red, and green. The cabin was a stark contrast to the rest of the ship.

"Wow!" said Cyrus, as he inspected the spotless and luxurious room. It didn't even smell musty. "This is nice. It must be the captain's cabin."

Justin was appalled, especially after having seen how the slaves were forced to live. "How can he live like this while so many people are suffering right beneath his feet?"

"Yeah!" said little Marcus, punching his fist into his hand. "Jesus said we should be kind to people."

Zak ruffled Marcus's hair. "I don't think the captain was listening when Jesus said that."

Ben and Helena looked around the cabin. "I'm afraid," said Ben, running a hand on the polished surface of a table, "he's like the man who built his house on the sand."

"Who?" said Marcus, scratching his head.

"A man Jesus talked about one day when he was

teaching in Capernaum. Sit down, all of you, and I'll tell you about him. It looks as though we'll be here for a while."

The children sat at Ben's and Helena's feet and Ben began, "As I said, Jesus was teaching in Capernaum when he said:

"'Everyone who listens to me and does something about it is like the man who builds his house on a rock. When winter comes,' he said, 'the house will stand up to storms because underneath the house is the rock.'

"Then he went on to say:

"'But whoever listens to me and does nothing is like a foolish builder. He builds his house on sand. Then when winter comes and the rains fall and the floods come and the winds blow, the house will come down with a tremendous crash.'"

Ben paused briefly to let the meaning of the story register when suddenly, a real crash made everyone jump. A painting had fallen off the wall as a furious Captain Hadrian entered his cabin. He was followed by his First Mate, laden with mops, buckets, and rags.

"Captain on deck!" shouted the First Mate.

Ben, Helena, and the children jumped up and snapped to attention. Captain Hadrian inspected them, eyeing them suspiciously.

"So these are the stowaways!"

Chapter 8

Jump to It

"Stowaways? Actually—" said Ben, but he was quickly interrupted.

"Quiet! I don't know why you're still on my ship, but I do know we're going into battle, and everyone on this ship pulls his weight!" Hadrian pointed to the utensils his First Mate was carrying and began barking orders.

"You," he said to Zak, "take that mop and bucket!"

"You, give water to the soldiers!" Justin jumped to it.

"You two!" Cyrus and Marcus looked anxiously at Captain Hadrian. "You stay here and clean!"

Then he turned to Ben. "And you, what do you do?"

"I'm a baker," Ben replied.

"Excellent!" Captain Hadrian pulled a bread roll from his pocket. "My cook makes the worst rolls in the Roman Navy." He bounced the brick-hard roll off the table. "Absolutely indestructible." Captain Hadrian turned to the First Mate and said, "Take him and those two to the galley at once!" He pointed at Helena and Anna.

The three, with Thastus the goat right behind them, followed the First Mate into the galley. They had never seen anything like it before. It was filthy! A fly-infested mess!

"Cook," said the First Mate, "this is Ben the baker, reporting for duty."

A burly, unshaven cook was bending over a large vat, scraping moldy leftovers from a plate into the scummy water.

"Quiet!" he spat. "I'm fixin' soup for the slaves!"

Helena covered her mouth with her hand and whispered to Ben, "Soup? I thought he was washing the dishes." Helena swallowed several times, trying to keep herself from being sick.

The cook picked up a scroll titled *Julius Childs' Cook Scroll* and spread it out on the counter. Running a greasy finger down the writing, he finally stopped at a recipe for "Slave Soup."

"Ah, here it is. Now that's one rotten tomato, one tiny slice of carrot." He fished a carrot out of the slime and cut it in half. He put one half back in the soup and the other in a dirty bowl.

Then he grabbed a live chicken from a cage. "And finally, fresh chicken." Cook dipped the squawking chicken into the water, then pulled it out. "Oops! Too much chicken. Can't have too much chicken. Always leave 'em wanting more. That's what the recipe says."

Scowling, the cook finally turned to Ben and Helena and scowled at them. "Now," he said, with a growl, "what do you want?"

"I'm supposed to help with the bread," said Ben,

31

smiling weakly at the slovenly Cook.

The cook dried his hands on his dirty apron and wiped his nose on his sleeve. Flies buzzed around his head. "Bread! Good, I could use some help."

He led Ben toward the baking area. The counter was caked with bits of dried dough. Dirty bowls were stacked at one end. A small barrel of flour sat on the floor.

"You know," said the cook, scratching his nose, "everybody loves my rolls. And they really came in handy against the Icenians!"

He loaded a roll into a dishrag slingshot and fired it at a pan, which was hanging over the oven. "Thonk!" went the roll, before ricocheting wildly around the galley. The gang ducked as it whizzed past them and flew out the door. A moment later they heard a soldier cry out, then they heard a splash. The cook laughed.

"I'll do my best to help," said Ben, as Helena stifled her laughter.

"Good," whispered the cook, darting a secretive look at Ben and Helena. "But remember, this here bread is not just a roll. It's a military secret!"

Ben tried to look properly impressed. "Your secret is safe with me, sir," he said. "Never fear!"

He and Helena exchanged glances. Only the glint in their eyes showed their amusement.

"Now," said Ben politely, "perhaps you could show me the way to your flour? And I will share with you my secret recipes!"

A dark and stormy night

A man lay on the doorstep

Captain Hadrian was cruel

"Do you know my father?" asked Justin

A show on deck

They were trapped on board

"Take this mop," said the captain to Zak

One of the slaves begged for a sip of water

"Four people were carrying a friend who could not walk"

They lowered their friend through the roof

The man got up and began to walk

Suddenly there was a crash

Thastus butted the door

Justin took the keys to the slave hold

Justin dived under water to free the slaves

The ship was sinking

Chapter 9

Nautical
Nero

Back at the port, Snivilus had been busy and was now ready to unveil his big surprise for Nero.

"Snivilus," snorted the Emperor, as Snivilus guided Nero down from his Imperial coach. "Whatever it is you have brought me here for, it had better be worth it."

"Oh it will, it will be," crowed Snivilus. "This way, Caesar, over to the quayside."

"A boat! You brought me all this way to see a boat."

"Ah!" said Snivilus, smugly. "But it is not just any boat. It is being refitted as Nero's Imperial Boat. After all, you are Emperor of the seas as well as the land in the Roman Empire."

"That I am. Well done, Snivilus. I am pleased," said Nero. "And I suppose the boat will be useful. I will be able to watch Hadrian feeding Christians to the sharks."

Snivilus positively glowed with pride. "Precisely, your Imperialness."

"I am doubly pleased, Snivilus. Perhaps you are not

quite the dolt I thought you were."

"Why, thank you, Caesar," Snivilus answered.

"Do we have a crew for this ship, Snivilus?"

"The best in all Rome. All hand picked, your greatness. The Imperial Navy. Ready and waiting as soon as—" Before Snivilus could finish his sentence Nero interrupted.

"Good, good. Doubly well done, Snivilus. Assemble the crew, we sail immediately."

"Immediately?" A cold shiver suddenly ran down Snivilus's spine.

"Come, come, you are not frightened of sailing, are you?" asked Nero, before turning and growling, "Snivilus! Call the crew now. That is an order! If we have the best crew in Rome, we will easily catch up with Hadrian. After all, some of his oarsmen are those unruly Christians. They'll be no match for the Imperial Navy."

Snivilus had heard that tone of voice before and knew Caesar meant business. "Aye, aye, excellent one. At once, your greatness. Immediately, your—"

"Snivilus, if I didn't know you better I would say you were playing for time. Jump to it, man!"

Snivilus jumped to it, but his feeling of woe would not go away.

Chapter 10

With
the Slaves

Deep in the hold of the ship, Justin held
a heavy bucket of water, waiting while a guard
took a long, refreshing drink. Around him, the slaves
rowed feverishly, their bare backs already shiny with
sweat and salt water.

"Boy! Over here," shouted another guard, standing
behind the slaves.

As Justin made his way to the other guard, the slave
named Caleb caught his eye. "Psst, just a little sip ..."

Justin paused, holding the ladle of water up to the old
slave's lips.

"Boy!" called the guard again. "I said over here!"

The guard walked over and grabbed Justin's arm,
roughly manhandling him away from Caleb, spilling the
water still left in the ladle.

* * *

In Captain Hadrian's cabin, Cyrus and Marcus were
fooling around when they should have been working.

35

Cyrus was wearing an oversized centurion's breastplate. It covered him from head to toe. All that could be seen of him were the top of his head with his two eyes peeping over the breastplate. His hands reached around the armor, struggling to clean the front.

Marcus fared no better. He had on a soldier's helmet. It was much too large, and he couldn't see a thing. As the ship rocked, both tumbled across the floor, crashing in a heap against the wall. They giggled at each other as they tried to stand up.

* * *

Up on deck, Zak looked like a wave-weary surfer, staggering back and forth across the deck with his mop and bucket.

"Stay … stay! Whoaaa!" said Zak to the bucket as it slid a few feet one way, then back the other way. The boat was beginning to rock and toss as the wind blew harder and dark clouds gathered overhead.

* * *

In the galley, the cook was showing Anna the fine art of making slave soup. "So you see," he said, as the boat rolled and the soup slopped from side to side in the big pot, "this potato doesn't have enough mold for slave soup. But this one is about right."

The cook held up a rotten potato, and Anna turned away from the awful smell.

Behind them, Ben opened the oven, and the wonderful

aroma of his fresh baked bread soon erased the smell of the rotten potato. The aroma also cast a spell on the sloppy cook. Ben wasn't known as the best baker in Rome for nothing.

"What's that … that smell?" asked the cook, as he looked dazedly at the rotten potato in his hand. Almost as if he was drawn by a magnet, the cook walked over to where Ben was cutting a loaf of fresh bread. Ben picked up a piece and waved it beneath the cook's nose.

"It's not supposed to smell like that," the cook said, breathing in deeply to get a better whiff of the bread.

Anna slid a chair behind the cook, and he sat down slowly, dreamily.

As Helena buttered a hot slice of bread, she said, "Perhaps you should taste it and tell us what we've done wrong."

"But I've got … so much … to do." The cook closed his eyes, mesmerized by the enchanting smell of Ben's bread.

"We can finish in the galley for you. Take your time with the bread," Ben said.

The cook started gobbling down the bread. His mouth full, he said, "Yes, mmm! Yes, good idea."

* * *

A guard cracked a whip over the slaves as they rowed in a steady rhythm.

"Faster," the guard yelled. "Faster." The beat from the tempo drum increased.

As the slaves tried to pick up the pace, old Caleb, exhausted, collapsed on the floor.

Justin ran to him and gave him some water.

"I told you to stay away from him!" growled the guard angrily, picking Justin up by one arm.

"He's dying of thirst!" cried Justin.

"If he doesn't row, he'll die of much worse!"

"Then I'll take his place." Justin stood up straight and looked the guard in the eye.

"Take his place?" The guard looked Justin up and down, making him feel two feet tall. "Hah!"

"At least until he is better." Justin looked anxiously at the cruel guard. His bravery had vanished.

"This I have got to see! Go ahead, little man! Row!"

Justin took Caleb's seat in the last row, beside Andrew, and struggled to pull the huge oar in time with the others.

"Well, gentlemen," said the guard to the rest of the slaves. "Since we have new blood, you should have no trouble doing attack speed for a while. Shall we?"

He cracked the whip and as the tempo drummer increased the pace, Andrew angrily turned to Justin. "You're just trying to get us killed, aren't you!"

Justin was visibly shaken. "I … I was only trying to help."

"If you want to help, keep silent and row," Andrew growled.

* * *

In the galley, Ben had no idea of Justin's plight. He was busy preparing a large vat of soup while Helena chopped up fresh vegetables and meat.

The cook was still seated near Anna, who pulled more pans of fresh bread out of the oven.

"Is this batch any better?" asked Anna coyly.

"No. No better. It's still too soft!" said the cook, tearing a loaf of bread in two. "Please pass more butter."

* * *

The black sky rumbled as the storm continued to howl outside. Below the main deck, a guard inspected the chains on the slaves, going from one to the next. Andrew's chain was loose, and he roughly secured it to the main chain that tied the slaves together.

When he got to Justin, he noticed that the boy wasn't chained.

"Don't worry about the boy," said the other guard.

"It must be nice to be free," Andrew said to Justin after the guard had walked on.

"As a matter of fact," replied Justin, "it's not so great being free when your dad's a slave and you don't know where he is."

Andrew looked at Justin, but gave no reply.

* * *

In the captain's cabin, Cyrus and Marcus were still cleaning the armor and helmets. But as the storm picked up and the waves grew bigger, they began rolling around the cabin like wooden balls. The ship pitched steeply to one side, and Cyrus crashed into a wall. A ring of keys fell on his head, then slid to the floor beside him.

* * *

The slaves continued to row for all they were worth, sweating and grunting. Andrew watched Justin struggling and, reluctantly, offered some advice. "Keep your back straight and bend your knees."

Justin looked at him but was too tired to say a word. Doing as he had been told, he soon got into the rhythm and rowed with the others against the storm.

Chapter 11

Supper for Stouticus

Back in Rome, at the port, while Nero waited in his carriage for the Imperial Navy to arrive, Snivilus was arguing with the Captain of the new ship.

"What do you mean he wants to set sail immediately?" asked the Captain.

"What Nero wants, Nero gets," said Snivilus. "We sail immediately. I have summoned the crew. They are on their way."

"But the ship is not ready yet," argued the Captain. "You know that. You asked me for a new ship, and I offered you this one. But it's still being built. Look at her. The carpenters are only just getting ready to put the main mast in. It has only just arrived. It will be days before it is finally ready to sail."

"Days!" wailed Snivilus. "But Nero wants to sail today. Right away!"

"Well," said the Captain, as he began giving the

signal to hoist the main mast into the air, "do you want to be responsible for sending the Emperor of Rome out to sea in a leaky, half-built boat?"

Snivilus wailed again: "Now he will feed me to the lions, for sure. And you too, I have no doubt. We must do something." Snivilus was frantic. His great plan to please Caesar was already sinking.

"What do you suggest?" asked the Captain.

But Snivilus had no idea; all he could think about was Nero's reaction when he told him the truth.

Just then, the Imperial crew, marching at double time, turned the corner into the port and approached the ship.

"Snivilus!" screamed Nero impatiently, as he spied the crew from his carriage. "That's the crew now. Let's get on board. And you," shouted Nero to the ship's carpenters, "get that mast erected, or it's the lions for all of you."

"Oh no!" groaned Snivilus.

As he spoke, the ship's carpenters began nervously pulling at the ropes to hoist the new mast over towards the hull. "Take it nice and easy," called the foreman, "and keep a tight grip of those ropes. One slip and we could lose it, and I don't fancy being a lion's breakfast."

Snivilus watched in vain as the mast swung high over everyone's heads. But just as he had resigned himself to telling Nero the bad news, that the boat wasn't sea-worthy, something very unexpected happened. Quite by chance, Snivilus was favored by the bumbling assistance of Stouticus.

Stouticus was the worst soldier in the whole of the Roman Army. He had only room for one thought at a time, and that thought was usually food. It was his day off, and he had been fishing.

"Mmm!" he said, as he waddled away from the water's edge. "I like a nice piece of fish, and these will do nicely for my supper." Stouticus held up a couple of large mackerel and admired them. Just then a huge white seagull swooped down and made a grab for one of the fish.

"Oh no, you don't! You're not having my supper!" shouted Stouticus, in a panic, and drawing his sword, he waved it frantically at the bird.

"Hoi! Watch that sword!" shouted the foreman, as he ducked out of the way. But he was too late. As Stouticus swiped at the seagull, he sliced straight through the rope the carpenters were using to winch the mast onto the ship.

"Look out!" cried Snivilus.

"Idiots!" snarled Nero.

But the shouting was all in vain. The mast, as true as a marksman's arrow, dropped from the winch and sliced straight through the boat.

"Idiots! I'm surrounded by fools and idiots. Look at my boat! My beautiful boat," wailed Nero, as his new ship, with a gaping great hole in its hull, slipped slowly under the water.

"Oh dear," smirked Snivilus, as the last of the ripples faded. "Nero won't be able to sail after all."

* * *

Chapter 12

In the Soup

After hours of being tossed to and fro in the storm, the ship finally began riding more evenly. The rain stopped. The storm had finally broken. The sails were hoisted, and the slaves were allowed to pull in their oars. They were all exhausted, including Justin. The guards unchained them and herded them back down into the ship's hold. But as they descended into the hold, Ben and the others were waiting.

"That smell ... it ... it's wonderful," said Caleb.

The others, sniffing the air, murmured their approval.

"What is it?" asked another.

Ben whisked the lid off the large soup pot. "It's dinner! Come eat!"

The grateful slaves gathered around as Helena passed out bowls. Soon the hardships of slavery and the poor conditions in the hold were forgotten. It was a scene of merriment as the slaves began their first decent meal in a long, long time.

After finishing the meal, the slaves sat in groups, chatting for a time before going to sleep. Some had gathered around Ben. Pressing closer to him, straining to hear, they were held captive by the story he was telling.

"And then Jesus went back to Capernaum," said Ben. "People had heard all about him, so they came from all around the countryside to listen to his stories.

"One day, he was in a house, teaching the people about God's way, when a group of people came to the door. They were carrying a paralyzed man on a pallet. They tried to get in, but they couldn't. The place was packed. No one could get in or out.

"Then one man pointed to the roof. The others climbed up and began taking the roof apart.

"While Jesus continued teaching, they removed the roof, tied ropes onto the pallet, then lowered their paralyzed friend into the house. Right in front of Jesus.

"Well, when Jesus saw the trust these four people had in him to help their friend, he turned to the paralyzed man and said, 'Young man, your sins are forgiven.'

"Some of the onlookers were shocked and began whispering to each other. 'Why does this man say things like that?' said one. 'Only God can forgive sins.'

"Jesus turned to them and said, 'Is it easier to say to this man "Your sins are forgiven" or "Get up, take your mat, and walk"?'

"No one replied, and Jesus, to prove to the doubters that he did have the power to forgive sins, turned to the man and said, 'Get up, take your mat, and go home.'

"Everyone in the house went silent. The man, looking amazed, stood up, picked up his mat, and tossed it to his friends. Then, hesitantly, a bit wobbly at first, he took a few steps. The crowd made room for him as he walked out of the house and down the street to his home.

"How that crowd must have cheered," said Ben. "This was an incredible and amazing thing they had seen."

The slaves smiled at Ben. "That is an amazing story," one said.

"And an amazing dinner," said another.

As Justin was gathering up the bowls, Andrew pulled him aside. "Justin," he said gruffly, as was his manner.

Justin was surprised to see that Andrew was holding out his hand.

"The name's Andrew," he said. "You did a good thing, rowing for Caleb today. I'm sure wherever your father is, he would be very proud of you."

Justin smiled and clasped Andrew's outstretched hand. "I'm not even sure he's still alive."

Andrew gave Justin a knowing smile and squeezed his hand.

Suddenly there was a shrill clanging of the ship's bell. It was the battle alarm. Above them, the hatch burst open.

"All slaves to oars!" roared a guard.

The slaves began to scramble up the ladder.

"What's happening?" Cyrus asked a passing slave.

"We're under attack!"

Andrew looked out of a porthole. "It's a rebel ship!"

"And it's heading right for us!" shouted Zak.

The children gulped with fear as they looked through portholes at the massive rebel ship, its deck lanterns glowing in the darkness, moving silently toward them under battle speed.

Chapter 13

Collision

The rebel ship cut through the waves, throwing water to either side as it bore down on Captain Hadrian's ship.

"Port oars in!" commanded Captain Hadrian. "Bring her hard about. Now!"

The guard cracked his whip and repeated Captain Hadrian's orders to the slaves. "Port oars in!" Andrew and the others on the port side of the ship struggled to pull their oars in so they wouldn't get broken if the rebel ship rammed them.

Captain Hadrian stood on the bridge as the rebel ship kept coming, closer and closer.

There was an almighty crunch as the two ships collided. The rebel ship hit Hadrian's ship a glancing blow, then slid alongside before moving away. Captain Hadrian watched as the rebel ship moved smoothly through the water until it was about two ship lengths away, this time on the starboard side.

"To port! To port! Now!" Captain Hadrian shouted

angrily as the rebel ship, appearing to be unhurt from the collision, circled menacingly.

When the two ships had collided, Ben and the others were thrown to the deck in the hold, and slid in the slimy water. They could see jagged holes in the hull and splinters clinging to the wooden planks. Water sprayed in through the cracks.

One level above them, where the slaves were rowing, a guard stuck his head out of a porthole and yelled, "Captain, some of the oars were damaged in the last pass!"

Then the lookout, clinging high up on a mast, shouted, "They're coming back around!"

Captain Hadrian looked on helplessly as the rebel ship completed its turn and headed straight for his ship.

"Prepare to be boarded!" he commanded.

Soldiers echoed the command on deck, as shields and spears were handed out.

Chapter 14

Into Battle

Down in the hold, Ben, Helena, and the rest of the gang peered through the portholes on the undamaged side of the ship and saw no sign of the rebel ship.

"Where did it go?" asked Anna.

"I don't know, I can't see it," Cyrus said.

Zak, who had made his way to the other side of the ship, yelled, "I can! Here it comes!"

Just then there was a horrendous crashing sound as the bow of the rebel ship ripped through the hull.

Zak ran as fast as he could to escape, but he wasn't fast enough. The bow of the rebel ship snagged on his tunic and lifted him into the air.

"Ahhhhh!" he screamed.

Ben reached up for Zak as he dangled in midair. "Give me your hand, Zakkai!"

But just before Ben could grab Zak's hand, the rebel ship backed out, taking Zak with it. Water flooded through the gaping hole in the hull, and Ben and the others were washed back to the deck. Now the water was getting deeper. Quickly.

"Ben! Ben!" shouted Zak.

"Hold on, Zak!" yelled Ben, spluttering as he struggled to stay afloat in the rising water. "We'll get to you somehow!"

* * *

While Ben and the others struggled to get out of the flooding hold, up on deck the soldiers were having their own problems. The freed slaves from the rebel ship had jumped aboard and were fighting, man to man, swords clashing. Some of the slaves were setting fire to anything that would burn. The ship's sails were the first to go up in flames.

* * *

Zak, who was still hanging from the bow of the rebel ship, had gone unnoticed. Having partially freed his tunic, he struggled to pull himself up onto the ship. He reached up onto the gangplank just as rebels were running across to board Captain Hadrian's ship.

"Hello!" shouted Zak. "Can anyone give me a hand?"

Not hearing him, a rebel stepped on his fingers. Zak yelped like a puppy. "Ouch! That's not what I had in mind."

* * *

Back in the hold, Ben and the others were faring no better. The level of the water was rising rapidly, and the gang had taken refuge in the huge, empty soup cauldron. But if they did not get out soon, the water would soon reach the ceiling, and they would drown.

Luckily, Justin managed to free a grate on the ceiling, and after Ben climbed through, he pulled them up, one by one.

"Come on," he said. "Quickly. We can make it through the galley!"

They all ran down a passageway on the lower deck, into the galley. There they saw Thastus, the goat, contentedly chewing a bag of grain.

"Good old Thastus," said Ben. "He's as calm as can be."

The children began untying the billy goat, but a faint knocking sound distracted Justin.

"Shh! Listen!"

Voices could be heard shouting, "Help! Help us!"

Chapter 15

Sinking Slaves

Standing very still in the galley, they heard again the cries of "Help! Help!"

"Who is it?" asked Anna.

"The slaves! They're still locked in chains! They'll drown!" cried Justin.

"We can't unlock the chains," Ben said, his forehead wrinkling in a frown. "We don't have the keys!"

Cyrus suddenly remembered how the ring of keys had fallen on his head when he was cleaning Captain Hadrian's cabin. "The keys! I saw some keys in the captain's cabin!"

Justin looked at Ben, who needed no urging. "Let's go!" Ben said.

* * *

On the main deck, the fighting continued to rage. The main mast was burning like a giant torch. The rebel ship bobbed alongside, but the fighting was all on Captain Hadrian's ship.

Ben and the gang made their way through the chaos, then back down to the captain's cabin. Cyrus turned the handle on the door. He pushed. Nothing happened.

His disappointment was obvious. "It's locked!"

Justin, Cyrus, and Ben slammed against the door a few times with their shoulders.

"It won't budge!" Justin cried.

Just as he said that, Cyrus heard a noise behind them. "Look out!" he cried.

Ben and Justin turned around to see Marcus, sitting on Thastus's back, just as Thastus charged at full speed toward the door.

"Ramming speed!" shouted Marcus, hanging on to the goat's collar.

Justin, Cyrus, and Ben dived out of the way as Thastus crashed through the door and disappeared into the captain's cabin, carrying Marcus with him. They were followed, hastily, by Cyrus.

"Well done, Marcus!" said Justin.

Cyrus emerged from the cabin, clutching the bunch of keys. "Got them!"

"Good," said Ben. "Helena, quickly, you and the kids have to get onto the other ship. Justin and I will see to the slaves."

Helena kissed Ben and, giving him a loving look, said, "Be careful."

"We will be. Don't worry. Let's go, Justin."

They all ran down the corridor and climbed up to the

deck. Ben and Justin headed for the slaves trapped below deck, and Helena and the other kids ran to the side of the ship.

"Helena! This way!" shouted Zak, who was waving at them from the deck of the rebel ship.

Chapter 16

Ben, Look Out!

As Helena and the kids made their getaway, Ben was distracted by a creaking and cracking sound. He looked up just in time to see the crossbeam on the burning mast snap.

"Ben, look out!" shouted Zak.

Ben grabbed Justin and dodged out of the way of the falling beam.

"Oh, no!" said Justin.

The crossbeam had blocked the entryway to the lower deck where the slaves were chained. The cries for help grew more frantic as the ship began to sink.

"Quickly," said Ben. "Give me a hand."

Ben and Justin struggled to move the crossbeam, but it was no use. It was jammed solid.

Justin saw a small opening between the splintered wood and the door. "I think I can make it," he said. "If I can just get that door open."

He crouched down and began to squeeze through.

"Easy, easy," said Ben, rubbing his own large paunch.

He knew there would be no chance of his joining Justin. The boy would have to free the slaves by himself—alone.

With a final twist of his slim body, Justin managed to squeeze through. As he swung open the door, light spilled down on the slaves. Held together by their chains, they were crying out for help. The whole ship was listing, and Justin had to hang on as he made his way down the stairs and waded into the water. The water was already waist-high on some of the slaves, up to the shoulders of those on the port side. He saw the large hole in the hull where the water was pouring in. He knew they didn't have much time.

"Justin!" cried Andrew.

"Andrew, I have the keys!" Justin shouted, waving the keys in the air.

Andrew smiled and shouted, "Start with them!" He was pointing to the other side of the ship. The slaves on the port side were now up to their necks in water—and it was still rising rapidly.

Justin took a deep breath and dived into the salty water. He swam along the floor, feeling for the chain which ran through the leg irons of the slaves. Finding it, he followed the chain to the padlock and, still holding his breath, fumbled with the padlock, trying several keys. Nothing fit. He could no longer hold his breath. Blowing out through his mouth, Justin pushed against the deck with his feet and popped to the surface, gulping for air.

Then, filling his lungs with air, he dove down to the

lock. There was one more key. It slipped into the lock. Justin turned the key and heard a click. The lock was open. He pulled it off the chain and once again erupted to the surface, gasping for air, the padlock held high above his head.

The slaves all cheered and began pulling the chain out of their leg irons.

*   *   *

Up on deck, Ben and Zak helped the freed slaves through the narrow opening of the partially blocked door. Unlike Ben, the slaves had grown so thin on their slave diet that they were all skinny enough to slip through. Thick smoke now filled the air, and the ship was listing heavily to port, sitting much lower in the water.

*   *   *

Justin moved through the flooded room to the starboard side, the high side. The slaves there, still locked in their chains, were choking on the heavy smoke in the air and on the water that was now at chin level.

"Everybody hold on!" shouted Justin.

"Hurry!" spluttered old Caleb, as he stretched his neck, trying to keep his head out of the water. "The lock, it's over there," he said, pointing to an area a few rows ahead of him.

Justin took three or four more deep breaths, then dove. Once again, he felt his way along the chain, searching for the second padlock. Because of Caleb's help, he soon found it, inserted the key, and with another click, it opened.

As the slaves began pulling their legs irons free, Justin looked around nervously. The smoke in the air was choking him and the ship seemed to be listing more. It was harder to walk without sliding and slipping into the deeper water.

The ship, Justin knew, was about to go down.

"Andrew!" shouted Justin. He could see the slave struggling to get free.

"Justin, save yourself!" Andrew cried.

* * *

On deck, Ben helped old Caleb to get through the narrowed doorway. The deck was brightly lit by the burning mast. Caleb, unused to the light, shielded his eyes. Suddenly, there was a loud creaking as the area around Ben grew even brighter and hotter. Caleb looked up through his fingers in time to see the mast collapsing toward them.

Ben grabbed Caleb, and he and the other slaves dived out of the way just in time. The burning mast crashed through the deck, dropping into the flooded area that the slaves had just left. It landed smack between Justin and Andrew, throwing water over both of them and pinning Andrew's chain to the floor.

Justin, rubbing his eyes to clear them of the smoke and

water, saw Andrew being pulled under the water by the mast.

"Andrew!" shouted Justin, climbing over the still-smoking mast and diving down to where Andrew was.

Andrew was struggling to pull his chain free, but the mast was too heavy. He couldn't budge it. Justin swam over to help, but the man shoved him away, trying to get him to leave. Justin ignored him and grabbed hold of the chain. Together they pulled.

*   *   *

Ben and Zak and the last of the freed slaves jumped over the side of the doomed ship.

"Come on, Justin," said Ben softly, holding his breath and treading water to stay up. His eyes searched the ship anxiously as he prayed for Justin to appear.

There was a loud crack as the ship sank lower. A gurgling sound was heard as the sea filled pockets of air in the sinking ship.

"Come on!" Ben yelled to Zak, who had jumped in the water to help. The two swam toward the sinking ship, while Helena and the others, safe on the rebel ship, looked on anxiously.

Captain Hadrian's huge ship gave a sudden roll and then, in a surge of froth and bubbles, sank into the dark sea. All was quiet.

Chapter 17

Shark Fin Soup

For a brief moment, the surface of the water looked serenely calm. Ben and Zak looked at each other, then studied the water around them. They saw nothing but the ever-increasing circular ripples in the water moving out from where the ship had disappeared.

Then, just as all seemed lost, there was an eruption of bubbles, followed by loud gasping for air.

Ben and Zak heard the cheer from the rebel boat. Then they saw two heads, Justin and Andrew, who had surfaced right where the Roman Navy ship had been.

They were free.

*   *   *

The crew of the rebel ship plucked the last of the freed slaves out of the water and, as night fell, Ben and the others were seated, wrapped in blankets, around a fire on deck. Caleb was already in the middle of a story.

"… and it was all thanks to young Justin, here."

"Well done, lad," said one of the freed slaves.

"I mean, there we were," said Caleb, "the sea was pouring in, up to our throats, when suddenly the door burst open and in comes this boy with a fistful of keys."

Justin smiled at the group and listened awhile longer. Then he stood up and walked away from the crowd and Caleb's story, looking sadly up at the night sky. The stars blinked softly in the moonlight as a light breeze filled the ship's sails.

"Justin," said a gentle voice in the darkness. It was Andrew. He was standing with the captain of the rebel ship. "I said I didn't know your father, but here is someone who does. Justin, I'd like you to meet our Captain Micah."

The captain smiled at Justin. "So you're the son of Joshua Ben Judah."

"You know him?" said Justin hopefully, looking up at the captain. He missed his father so much, and even the mention of his name filled him with sorrow. His eyes were brimming with tears.

Captain Micah, sensing Justin's sadness, crouched down and looked into the boy's eyes. A tear slid down one cheek.

Admiration spread across the captain's face. "Know him! I'll never forget him! Your father saved my life. Last I heard he'd escaped from his ship and was searching for your mother on the farms of Carthage. I've never met a braver man—and you're just like him."

Later, Ben, Helena, and the others looked on proudly as Captain Micah and Justin strolled along the deck, Captain Micah telling Justin more stories of his father.

*   *   *

Out of sight, but not far off, Hadrian, his first mate, and the cook floated on a wooden hatch cover, paddling with their hands. The night was lit by a bright yellow moon.

"I said, after them! After them!" Captain Hadrian was still the captain, still giving orders. Turning to the cook he said, "What's for dinner, by the way?"

A shark circled their flimsy craft and eyed them hungrily. "Uh! It looks like we are," said the cook nervously.

The captain and first mate looked horrified. They began to paddle frantically, looking back every now and then at the shark's fin following behind them.

*   *   *

Ahead of them, the rebel ship, with Ben and Helena and the children safely aboard, sailed peacefully along the silvery moon path that shimmered and glinted on the sea. They were heading home—together.